OUR DOG BENJI

PETE CARTER

JAMES HENDERSON

EK

I love our dog Benji.
Sometimes I think I'd like
to be more like him.
He eats almost anything
and everything. I'm not
that adventurous.

He eats Brussels
sprouts, mushrooms —
raw or cooked — yucky
tomatoes, olives, even
slimy avocado.

In the park, he eats grass
and daffodils, and pretends
he's hungry if anyone
is eating ice cream ...
That, I understand.

Every morning, he hurries to the kitchen in case the fridge exploded overnight. When he finds it hasn't, he searches the floor carefully for crumbs instead.

During meal times at home, he takes up position under the table, hoping guests are either messy or fussy.

If the gate is open, off he goes,
looking for food and company.

Once we found him
sitting on a builder's
knee, sharing his
homemade sandwiches.

Benji likes to attend parties next door, enjoying posh food and conversation before politely being sent home.

He loves a bone, and will bury
it in a flowerpot, forget it,
remember it, then bury it again.

In the summer, bugs become
fair game — noisy, dozy and
perhaps just a little crunchy.

When we visit our cousins, he eats
green apples straight from the tree.
His tummy becomes round like a barrel
and makes loud, rumbling sounds.
Even he can't stand the smell!

I don't think I'll ever be
quite as adventurous as Benji.
I won't eat flowers in the
park or bones or bugs, and
I'll drink water from a glass,
not a bowl.

But I will eat fruit and
vegetables, and my
meals at meal times
— although I might
have mine at the table.

I won't eat everything, though. There's one thing not even Benji will eat. And neither will I.

Celery.